This
Korky Paul
DICTURE BOOK
BELONGS TO:

Endpapers by Aoub Benkacem Dib aged 11.
Thank you to Botley Primary School, Oxford
for helping with the endpapers.

To Mum, and in memory of Tess the dog – J.L.
To Ian Hamilton Gordon – K.P.

OXFORD
UNIVERSITY PRESS

Great Clarendon Street, Oxford OX2 6DP
Oxford University Press is a department of the University of Oxford.
It furthers the University's objective of excellence in research, scholarship,
and education by publishing worldwide in

Oxford New York

Auckland Cape Town Dar es Salaam Hong Kong Karachi
Kuala Lumpur Madrid Melbourne Mexico City Nairobi
New Delhi Shanghai Taipei Toronto

With offices in

Argentina Austria Brazil Chile Czech Republic France Greece
Guatemala Hungary Italy Japan Poland Portugal Singapore
South Korea Switzerland Thailand Turkey Ukraine Vietnam

Oxford is a registered trade mark of Oxford University Press
in the UK and in certain other countries
© Text copyright Jonathan Long 1992
© Illustrations copyright Korky Paul 1992
The moral rights of the author and illustrator have been asserted
Database right Oxford University Press (maker)
First published as The Dog That Dug by The Bodley Head Children's Books 1992
Reissued by Oxford University Press 2008

2 4 6 8 10 9 7 5 3 1

British Library Cataloguing in Publication Data

Data available

ISBN: 978-0-19-276351-8 (paperback)

Printed in China

www.korkypaul.com

The Dog Who Could Dig

Written by Jonathan Long

OXFORD
UNIVERSITY PRESS

Digger the dog was a bit of a clot.
He'd buried his bone and forgotten the spot.

He sniffed round the garden in search of his nibble,
till he sniffed something nice and started to dribble.

'That must be my bone,' he said, 'down in the muck.
I knew I would find it with a bit of good luck.'

So he stuck in his paws and he scratched and he dug,
till he found something hard and he gave it a tug.

When he opened his eyes, can you guess what he found?
It wasn't the bone that he'd left underground . . .

but a rotten brown shoe with a hole in the toe
that someone had dropped a long time ago.

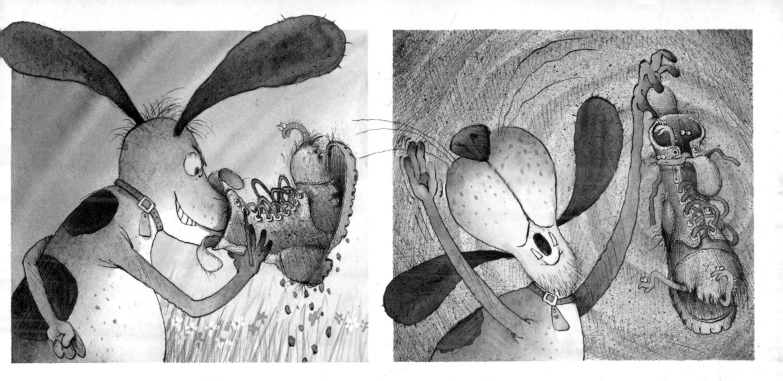

'I can't eat *that*,' Digger said with a frown,
'my bone must be deeper, I'll dig further down.'

So he stuck in his paws and he scratched and he dug,
till he found something else and he gave it a tug.

When he opened his eyes, can you guess what he found?
It wasn't the bone that he'd left underground . . .

but a coal-mining miner, all covered in soot,
very surprised to be tugged by the foot.

'Sorry,' said Digger, 'I do beg your pardon,
I didn't expect to find you in the garden!'

The miner was cross. 'You bad boy!' he hissed
as he grabbed Digger's throat in his big hairy fist.

'I can't eat *him*,' Digger said with a frown,
'my bone must be deeper, I'll dig further down.'

So he stuck in his paws and he scratched and he dug,
till he found something else and he gave it a tug.

It was terribly heavy and the dog had to battle,
but at last it came out with a shake and a rattle.

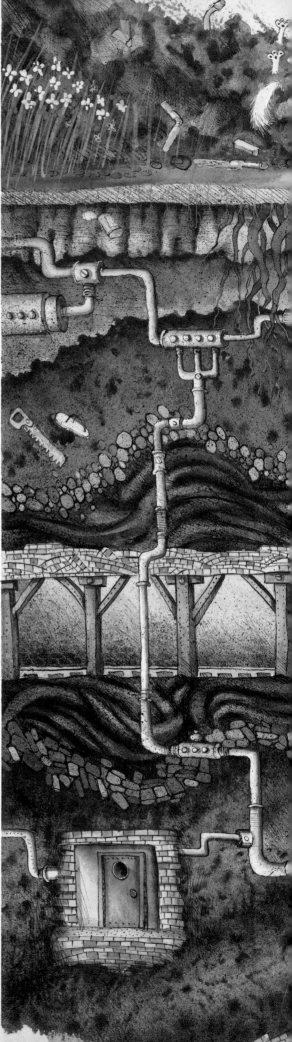

Can you guess what it was, the thing he had found?
A tubular train that chuffed underground!

With twenty-four carriages, all full of faces,
driven along by a man in red braces.

'What are you doing? This isn't my station!'
shouted the driver with great indignation.

'Sorry,' said Digger, 'I do beg your pardon,
I didn't expect to find you in the garden!'

'I can't eat *him*,' Digger said with a frown,
'my bone must be deeper, I'll dig further down.'

So he stuck in his paws and he scratched and he dug,
till he found something else and he gave it a tug.

But tugging it out was a terrible strain—
more of a strain than a tubular train.

And when it was out, can you guess what he'd found
buried away, deep under the ground?

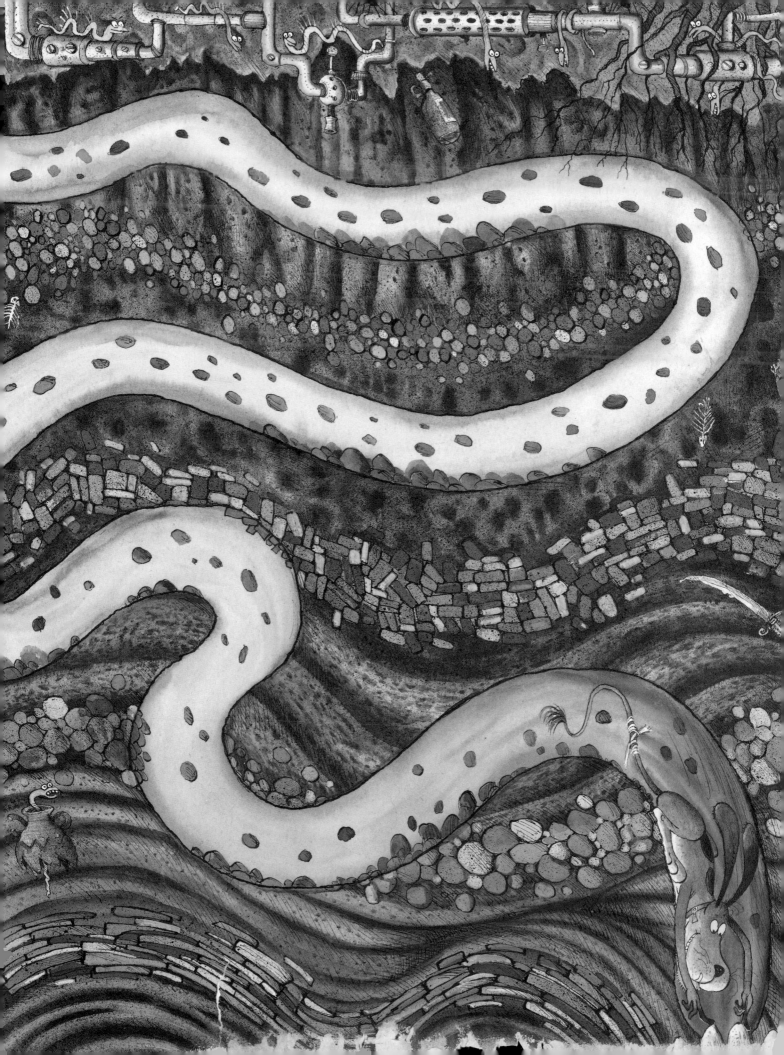

A bone at last! But it wasn't a single.
It was joined to some more and they all made a jingle.

There were big bones a-plenty and small ones galore
—all that was left of an old dinosaur.

'What a surprise,' Digger said with a smile,
'this pile of snacks will last quite a while.'

'Wait just one minute,' came a voice from aloft,
'those bones are rare and not to be scoffed.'

A smiling professor was over his shoulder
with little round specs and a shabby red folder.

'I'm hungry,' said Digger, 'those bones are my dinner.
If I don't eat them soon, I'll end up much thinner.'

'Look here,' said the prof, 'I'm not being funny,
give me those bones and I'll give you some money.'

'Great!' Digger said, showing one of his paws.
'Two million pounds and the bones will be yours!'

The prof scratched her head, saying 'um' and then 'ah',
then paid, and drove off with bones strapped to her car.

When she had gone, Digger went to the shops
and loaded his trolley with packs of pork chops.

He bought burgers, and steaks, and bangers in strings,
and hot spicy pies and fried chicken wings.

He invited his friends for a beautiful dinner,
where no-one had bones—and no-one got thinner!

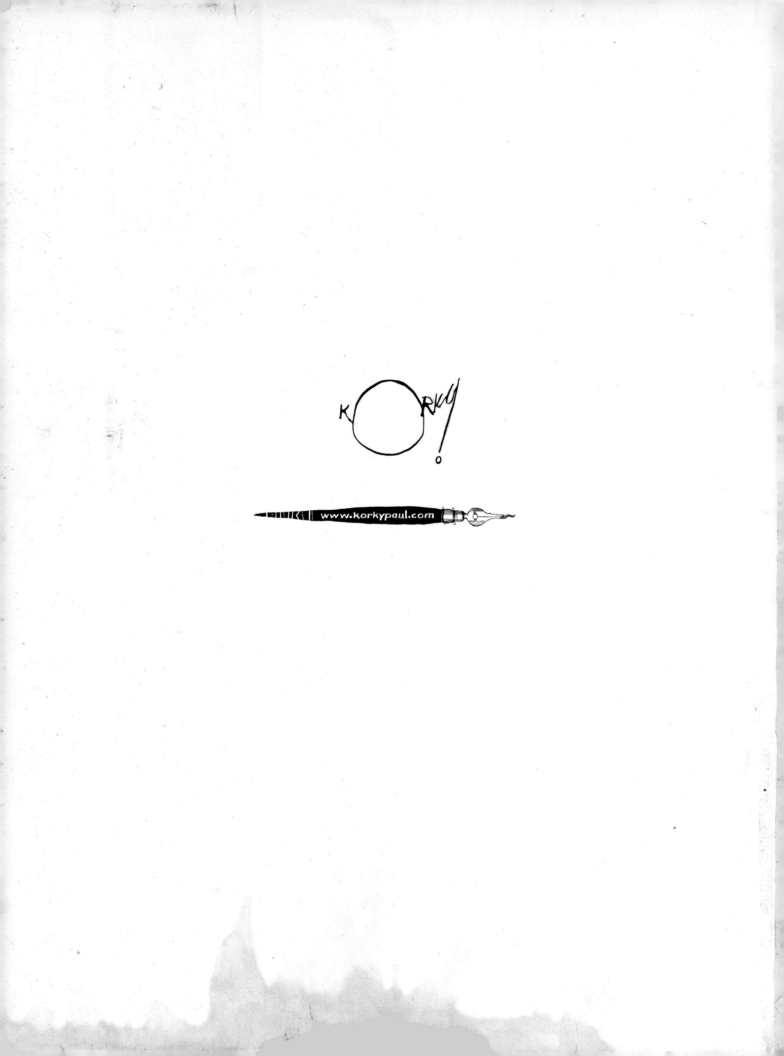